BIRDSONG

AUDREY WOOD

Drawings by

ROBERT FLORCZAK

Voyager Books

Harcourt, Inc.

San Diego   New York   London

Storyteller's Note

Birds are everywhere. Throughout the ages, poets, scholars, and common folk have been fascinated by the songs of birds. Sometimes their whistles, trills, and chirps have reminded people of words or sounds they know; those words or sounds are frequently used to describe the songs of many birds—and especially to help us identify birds in the wild.

For Rosalie Heacock and Estelle Busch, who know the birds' songs

—A. W.

In memory of my father, Henry Florczak

—R. F.

CAW-CAW-CAW—swaying on telephone wires, jaunty crows banter at dawn. Missy and Deni awaken to birdsong.

For breakfast Armando and Juan eat tortillas, eggs, and beans.
WHAT-CHEER, WHAT-CHEER, WHEAT-WHEAT-WHEAT—
saucy cardinals chatter just beyond their window.

Traffic lights change, taxis race down big city streets. Nearby there's a little park nestled among the skyscrapers. While Jordan and Elly play, gentle pigeons splash and make their cooing calls—COO-A-ROO, COO-A-ROO, COO-A-ROO.

In Yoshiko's flowering garden, tiny hummingbirds
battle bumblebees—CHIP-CHEE-CHEE—
and gather nectar from hibiscus blossoms.

Over the hills, down in the valley, Roger and Don begin their morning chores. BOB-O-LINK, BOB-O-LINK, SPINK-SPANK-SPINK— chattering bobolinks search for tasty morsels in plowed fields. DEAR-ME, DEAR-ME, DEAR-ME—swift goldfinches swoop over cornstalks ripening in the sun.

For a secret lunch, Jason's neighborhood friends meet in their tree house hideaway. CHICK-A-DEE-DEE-DEE—friendly chickadees flutter down to eat walnuts from their hands.

Where can the Miller twins go when the sun burns through
their T-shirts and their hot feet ache in their laced-up sneakers?
Down to the cool, moss-banked pond, where—GAWK! GAWK!—
startled herons fly up from water reeds with salamanders
dangling from their beaks.

The day is long, there's plenty of time for adventure, so Ranto and Navara paddle down a winding river. RICKITY-CRICK-CRICK, RICKITY-CRICK-CRICK—crafty kingfishers dive for insects, tadpoles, and silvery minnows.

Up in the mountains on wildflower trails, the air is thin and the summer moon shines pale in a sunny sky. Jim and Lou stop to listen—KEEYER, KEEYER, KEEYER. Fearless hawks soar high above their heads as they search for prey.

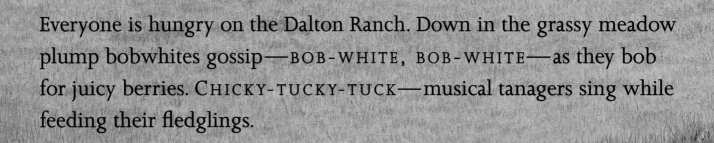

Everyone is hungry on the Dalton Ranch. Down in the grassy meadow
plump bobwhites gossip—BOB-WHITE, BOB-WHITE—as they bob
for juicy berries. CHICKY-TUCKY-TUCK—musical tanagers sing while
feeding their fledglings.

After a snack Bernard and Francis lie down for a nap, but
who can rest in the noisy bayou? YUCCA-YUCCA-YUCCA—
determined woodpeckers drum on dead tree limbs.
PUMPERLUNK, PUMPERLUNK—suspicious bitterns fuss while
hiding in cattails, and busy rails call—KEK-KEK-KEK—while
spearing crawdads.

As afternoon shadows stretch like long fingers on the forest floor, Alex chases Andrew. TEACHER-TEACHER-TEACHER—bossy ovenbirds scold from low branches.

Now the sun is down and the day is done. WHIP-POOR-WILL, WHIP-POOR-WILL—the worried whippoorwill calls Dahlia and Oren home.

WHO? WHO? WHO? Snug in their cozy beds, Daniel and Bruce are searching for sleep. WHO? WHO? WHO?—a questioning owl hoots from a hollow in her tree. The day ends as it began, with birdsong.

Requests for permission to make copies of any part of the work
should be mailed to the following address: Permissions Department,
Harcourt, Inc., 6277 Sea Harbor Drive, Orlando, Florida 32887-6777.

www.harcourt.com

First Voyager Books edition 2001
Voyager Books is a trademark of Harcourt, Inc.,
registered in the United States of America and other jurisdictions.

The Library of Congress has cataloged the hardcover edition as follows:
Wood, Audrey.
Birdsong/by Audrey Wood; illustrated by Robert Florczak.
p.   cm.
[1. Birdsongs—fiction.]   I. Florczak, Robert, ill.   II. Title.
PZ7.W846Bi   1997
[Fic]—dc20   95-45737
ISBN 0-15-200014-3
ISBN 0-15-202419-0 pb

A C E G H F D B

The illustrations in this book were done in Tombow water-based markers,
gouache, colored pencil, and opaque ink on blueprint paper.
The display type was set in University Bold.
The text type was set in Joanna.
Color separations by Bright Arts, Ltd., Singapore
Printed and bound by Tien Wah Press, Singapore
This book was printed on Arctic matte paper.
Production supervision by Sandra Grebenar and Ginger Boyer
Designed by Michael Farmer

The artist would like to thank the Los Angeles County Museum of Natural History, the
San Bernardino County Museum, the Los Angeles chapter of the Audubon Society, and
Anthony Mann for their assistance in his research.